This Little Tiger book belongs to:

Tiago

For Jack and Joe Mongredien,
and their very special Grandpa — S. M.

For Anne and Paul, with love — C. B.

LITTLE TIGER PRESS

1 The Coda Centre, 189 Munster Road, London SW6 6AW
www.littletiger.co.uk

First published in Great Britain 2011
by Little Tiger Press, London
This edition published 2012

Printed in China • LTP/1900/0840/0913

2 4 6 8 10 9 7 5 3

Before We Go To Bed

Sue
Mongredien

Cee
Biscoe

LITTLE TIGER PRESS

Barney and Grandpa Bear were tramping
home together after a busy day.
"What are we going to do next?"
Barney asked.
"Next?" chuckled Grandpa in surprise.
"Next, I think it's bedtime, Barney!"

Grandpa pulled off Barney's
boots with a heave-squelch-plop!
"Now, let's get you ready for bed,"
he said.

"Not yet, Grandpa!" Barney cried. "I ALWAYS have
a GIANT bowl of porridge before I go to bed. Yummy,
scrummy porridge, with sticky, licky honey!"

"Are you sure?" asked Grandpa.

"Oh, yes," said Barney.
"Come on!"

Barney showed Grandpa what a wonderful
porridge-maker he was.

"And now for the honey!" he cheered. But the
honey was runny . . . and it went EVERYWHERE.

"Whoops-a-daisy!" giggled Barney.

"Time for bed now," said Grandpa,
when Barney's tummy was full.

"But I ALWAYS have a big bubble bath before
I go to bed!" said Barney. "A splishy-sploshy
bath with my squeezy-squirty toys."

"I suppose you are a very sticky bear," Grandpa said, as Barney tipped in ALL the bubble bath with a glug-glug-gloop.

Barney splished and sploshed around in his bubble bath. The water went EVERYWHERE.

"Whoops-a-daisy!" giggled Barney.

"All clean!" Grandpa said. "It MUST be
bedtime now."

"But I'll NEVER get to sleep without a story,"
Barney said. "A spooky, scare-a-bear story
with horrible, hairy monsters."

"Is a spooky, scare-a-bear story a good idea before bed?" Grandpa wondered.

"Don't worry, Grandpa," said Barney. "It's only a story. It's not real."

So Grandpa read the story.

Afterward, Grandpa put the light
on again to make them both feel better.

"Maybe we shouldn't go
to sleep just yet," he said.

"I've got an amazing idea," said Barney.
"We could bounce on the bed! Shall we, Grandpa?"

Grandpa smiled.
"All right then," he said.
First they did little bear bounces.

Next they did bigger
bear bounces.

And then they did
great big,
springy-zingy,
boingy-bear
bounces!

Until ...

Crash! went the bed.

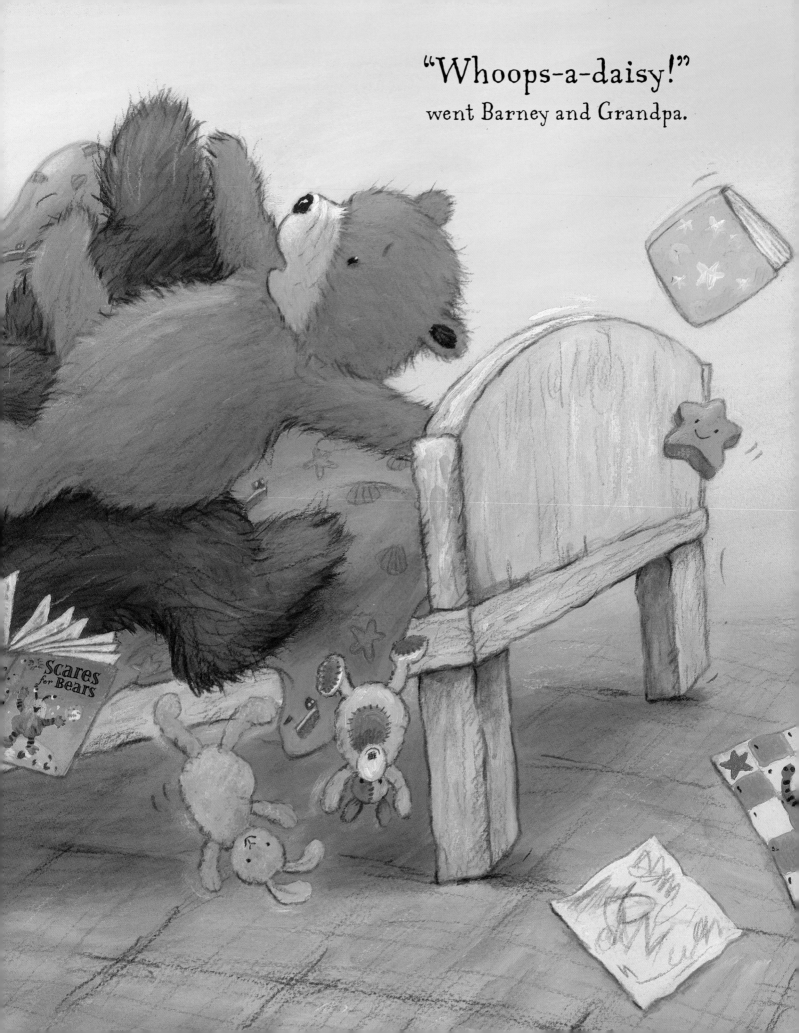

"Whoops-a-daisy!"
went Barney and Grandpa.

Barney watched as Grandpa mended
the bed. Then he gave a hu-u-uge
stretchy yawn.

"Sounds to me like it's definitely bedtime,"
said Grandpa, tucking Barney under
the covers.

"There's just one more thing I need,"
said Barney sleepily. "A super-squeezy,
squishy-squashy . . ."

"...BEAR HUG!"

Then both bears fell fast asleep
until the morning.